ONE MORE RIVER

A Noah's Ark Counting Song

Adapted and Illustrated
by JOAN PALEY

Megan Tingley Books
Little, Brown and Company
Boston New York London

ILLUSTRATOR'S NOTE

In the traditional biblical story of Noah's Ark, Noah learns that it is going to rain for a very long time, so he saves the animals by gathering them together in pairs aboard the Ark. In this book, things happen a little differently. "One More River" is a traditional spiritual that has been sung over and over in so many different ways — each singer may change it a little bit over the years. Although the song does tell the basic story of Noah and the Ark and the many days and nights of rain, the words reflect a counting theme as the animals board the Ark — can you count the animals as they come? You may notice that the animals aren't boarding in pairs! Count and sing along with Noah and the animals — you can even try to make up your own words as you go!

Text adaptation copyright © 2002 by Little, Brown and Company
Illustrations copyright © 2002 by Joan Paley

First Edition

Library of Congress Cataloging-in-Publication Data

Paley, Joan.
   One more river : a Noah's ark counting book / illustrated by Joan Paley. — 1st ed.
   p. cm.
   Summary: In this adaptation of a traditional spiritual, the animals enter Noah's ark in increasing numbers, from one elephant to ten hens.
   ISBN 0-316-60702-9
   1. Children's songs — Texts. [1. Noah (Biblical figure) — Songs and music. 2. Noah's ark — Songs and music. 3. Animals — Songs and music. 4. Counting. 5. Songs] I. Title.
   PZ8.3.P15655 On 2002
   782.25'3'0268
   [E]   00-065556

10 9 8 7 6 5 4 3 2 1

TWP

Printed in Singapore

The collage illustrations in this book are made up of shapes cut from different papers, which are painted with watercolor and textured with crayon, pastel, colored pencils, and oil paints. The layered shapes create a three-dimensional effect.

The text was set in Cantoria, and the display type was handlettered by the illustrator.

To Barbara, a true leader who challenged the "promise" and caused it to be kept; our heroine and model of what principles are, a rare distinction indeed.

With special thanks to Chip, the Chipster, and Loretta, who, with Barbara, have done and continue to do the impossible.

Love,
J. P.

ONE MORE RIVER

Rollicking

1. Old No - ah built a great big Ark, There's one more riv-er to

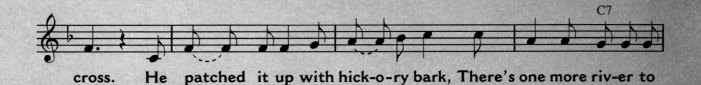

cross. He patched it up with hick-o-ry bark, There's one more river to

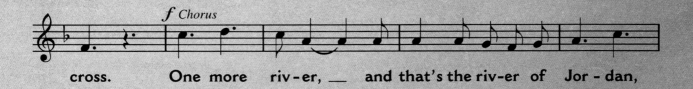

cross. One more riv-er, ___ and that's the riv-er of Jor - dan,

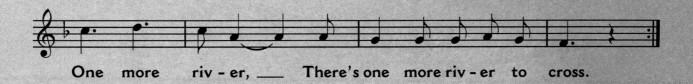

One more riv - er, ___ There's one more riv - er to cross.

Note: Although the chorus isn't repeated throughout this
book's pages, feel free to sing it after each verse!

Old Noah built a great big Ark,
There's one more river to cross,
He patched it up with hickory bark,
There's one more river to cross.
One more river—
And that's the river of Jordan,
One more river—
There's one more river to cross.

The Ark was anchored with a heavy rock,
There's one more river to cross,
Then Noah began to load his stock,
There's one more river to cross.

The animals went in one by one,
There's one more river to cross,
The elephant chewing a honey bun,
There's one more river to cross.

The animals went in two by two,
There's one more river to cross,
"Let's hop right in," said the kangaroo,
There's one more river to cross.

3 The animals went in three by three,
There's one more river to cross,
Baby bear said, "Please wait for me!"
There's one more river to cross.

4 The animals went in four by four,
There's one more river to cross,
The bulls stomped in, Noah waved for more,
There's one more river to cross.

5 The animals went in five by five,
There's one more river to cross,
Five fluffy llamas did arrive,
There's one more river to cross.

6 The animals went in six by six,
There's one more river to cross,
Noah laughed at the monkeys' tricks,
There's one more river to cross.

7 The animals went in seven by seven,
There's one more river to cross,
The flamingos' necks reached up to heaven,
There's one more river to cross.

8 The animals went in eight by eight,
There's one more river to cross,
The aardvark said, "Are we too late?"
There's one more river to cross.

9 The animals went in nine by nine,
There's one more river to cross,
The turtles came in slow green lines,
There's one more river to cross.

10 The animals went in ten by ten,
There's one more river to cross,
"We're the last ones in!" said the big fat hen,
There's one more river to cross.

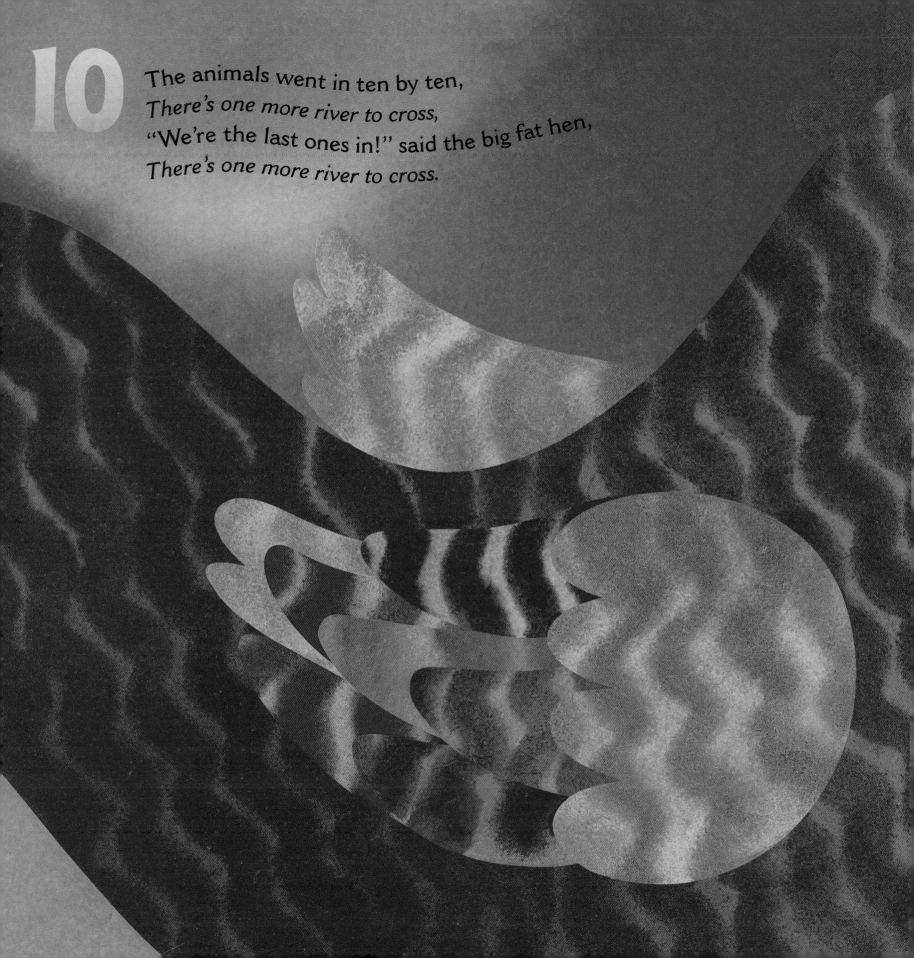

So then the voyage did begin,
There's one more river to cross,
Old Noah pulled the gangplank in,
There's one more river to cross.

For forty days and nights they sat,
There's one more river to cross,
Till they finally landed on Ararat,
Now there's no more river to cross.

No more river—
They've crossed the river of Jordan,
No more river,
Now there's no more river to cross!